Pink

A WOMEN'S
MARCH STORY

Written by **VIRGINIA ZIMMERMAN**
Illustrated by **MARY NEWELL DePALMA**

RP | KIDS
PHILADELPHIA

Grandma knits and knits and knits. I like the way the yarn feels—
soft and strong at the same time. But I don't know
how to knit. I think I'm too little.

I need some pink yarn.

"This yarn is baby pink.
I need grown-up pink for my next
project," Grandma says.

"Yes! I'm going to knit us some hats."

At the store, there are piles
and piles of pink yarn.

Pink like the roses in Grandma's garden.

Pink like the punch at snack time.

Pink like my cheeks
after I play in the snow.

"Women are making hats to wear and signs to wave at a Women's March in Washington, DC," Grandma says.

She says our whole family is going and that we'll all wear hats.

"Sometimes the men in charge disrespect women and make us feel small. But we are not small! We are strong and smart and beautiful, each in our own way. And all together, we are amazing," Grandma says.

"I feel small sometimes," I say.

"Grandma!" I say. "I want to knit
my own hat. Will you show me how?"

Grandma shows me how to
cast on and how to knit.

One by one, we make little loops with our yarn.
The loops stand together, shoulder to shoulder.

With the other needle, we draw our yarn
through each loop, making little hearts all in a row.
Grandma tells me this is called a knit stitch.

I make rows and rows of hearts. I drop one little stitch
by accident and make a big hole in my hat.

Knitting is hard!

Some days, we knit at the yarn store.

I knit a whole hat all by myself, and Grandma finishes enough hats for the entire family.

The night before the March, Grandma shows us a picture of her at another march a long time ago. She says, "Women wanted our government to pass a law saying that women and men have equal rights. There were lots and lots of people at that march, but no special hats."

Mama says women have done lots of amazing things since that march. Women are now astronauts and athletes, senators and scientists. But some men *still* make women feel small, so we are marching again.

Grandma, your hair was curly, just like mine!

At the bus station, there are so many hats.

Luke says, "I guess pink isn't just for girls."

"That's right," Dad says. "Our hats show our love and respect for Grandma, Mama, and Lina. They show how we stand together, shoulder to shoulder, right beside them."

love and respect

Now we begin to walk. Along the way,
we make some friends.

The crowd gets bigger and bigger.

Cars honk, and people wave.

Everyone is going in the same direction.

People chant while they walk:
"This is what democracy looks like!"

Today, democracy looks like
a parade of pink hats.

"We're here!" Mama says.

I can't see anything. I'm too small.

"Listen!" Grandma says. "I hear Gloria Steinem.
She spoke at my first march, too!"

Up high, all I can see is pink. Grown-up pink,
big-sister pink, and pink like my kitty's tongue. I feel like
one little stitch in a great big beautiful hat!

Look at us!
We are strong and smart and beautiful.
All together, we are amazing!

We stand shoulder to shoulder, hearts in a row, and march right down the middle of the street.

The March is over, but no one takes off their hats.

"I want the baby to know about the March," I say.

"You'll tell her," Grandma says.

"*And* I'll show her." I smile.

The very next day, I get to work.
I knit and knit and knit.

I finally get to meet my little sister.

She is amazing—just like me. And together,
we will make a better world.

author's note

On January 21, 2017, nearly one million people traveled to Washington, DC, for the Women's March. People who could not make the journey to the nation's capital marched in towns and cities throughout the United States and all over the world. Sources estimate that more than seven million people across the globe participated in Women's Marches on that day. People wanted to protest the negative comments about women made by the newly elected forty-fifth president of the United States, sworn into office the day before the March. They came together to celebrate women, all strong and beautiful in their own ways.

In Washington, DC, lots of famous and important people spoke and performed at the March. The youngest speaker was six-year-old Sophie Cruz, who delivered her inspiring speech in English and Spanish. Gloria Steinem (b. 1934), a feminist leader since the 1960s, said, "This is a day that will change us forever because we are together." Steinem also spoke at the 1978 march in support of the Equal Rights Amendment. Between 40,000 and 90,000 people attended that march. Around ten times as many were at the 2017 march.

The March was peaceful and hopeful and pink! Millions of marchers all over the world wore pink hats. Creators Jayna Zweiman and Krista Suh reacted to a hateful insult with defiant humor when they named these hats "pussyhats." They had the idea that a blanket of pink hats would make a powerful statement, and people unable to march could participate by making hats for other people to wear. Kat Coyle, the owner of the shop where Jayna and Krista took a crocheting class, designed a simple pattern so even beginners like Lina could make hats for themselves and others.

One type of hat may not be right for all people. Some chose to make different hats or not to wear hats at all, but with or without pink hats, millions of people all over the world came together on that day to say, "Women are strong. Women are beautiful. Each voice matters. And this is what democracy feels like."

Running Press Kids
Hachette Book Group
1290 Avenue of the Americas, New York, NY 10104
www.runningpress.com/rpkids
@RP_Kids

Printed in China

First Edition: January 2022

Published by Running Press Kids, an imprint of Perseus Books, LLC, a
subsidiary of Hachette Book Group, Inc. The Running Press Kids name and
logo is a trademark of the Hachette Book Group.

The Hachette Speakers Bureau provides a wide range of authors for
speaking events. To find out more, go to www.hachettespeakersbureau.com
or call (866) 376-6591.

The publisher is not responsible for websites (or their content) that are not
owned by the publisher.

Print book cover and interior design by Frances J. Soo Ping Chow.

Library of Congress Control Number: 2020939993

ISBNs: 978-0-7624-7389-2 (hardcover), 978-0-7624-7387-8 (ebook),
978-0-7624-7407-3 (ebook), 978-0-7624-7406-6 (ebook)

1010

10 9 8 7 6 5 4 3 2 1